Date: 10/13/16

Dropping In On...

Atlanta

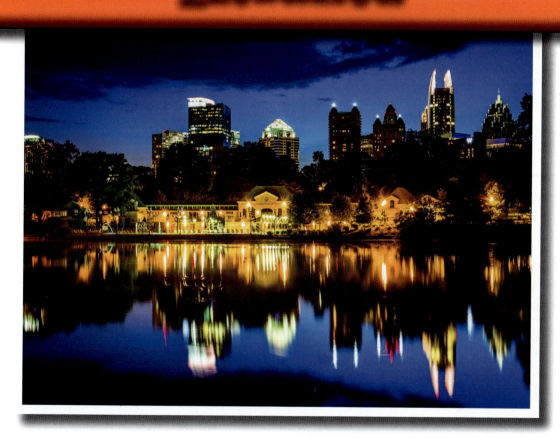

Jeff Barger

rourkeeducationalmedia.com

Scan for Related Titles
and Teacher Resources

Before Reading:

Building Academic Vocabulary and Background Knowledge

Before reading a book, it is important to tap into what your child or students already know about the topic. This will help them develop their vocabulary, increase their reading comprehension, and make connections across the curriculum.

1. *Look at the cover of the book. What will this book be about?*
2. *What do you already know about the topic?*
3. *Let's study the Table of Contents. What will you learn about in the book's chapters?*
4. *What would you like to learn about this topic? Do you think you might learn about it from this book? Why or why not?*
5. *Use a reading journal to write about your knowledge of this topic. Record what you already know about the topic and what you hope to learn about the topic.*
6. *Read the book.*
7. *In your reading journal, record what you learned about the topic and your response to the book.*
8. *After reading the book complete the activities below.*

Content Area Vocabulary
Read the list. What do these words mean?

capital
effects
executive
exhibits
grace
hub
institutions
multicultural
population
recreation

After Reading:

Comprehension and Extension Activity

After reading the book, work on the following questions with your child or students in order to check their level of reading comprehension and content mastery.

1. *Why are so many streets named Peachtree in Atlanta? (Summarize)*
2. *Why was the railroad so important to the city in its early days? (Infer)*
3. *What influential people in U.S. history lived there? (Asking questions)*
4. *What do you find most interesting about Atlanta's history? (Text to self connection)*
5. *Why is The Varsity such a popular place? (Asking questions)*

Extension Activity

Imagine you are the mayor of Atlanta, and the Great Atlanta Fire of 1917 has just ended. What would you do to rebuild the city? What types of things would be most important to the people who lived there?

Table of Contents

Where in the World? 4

The End is the Beginning 6

The Civil War 9

On the Move 11

Famous Atlantans.................15

City of Learning 19

Games People Play 20

Food, Fun, and Festivals 25

Timeline 29

Glossary 30

Index...................................31

Show What You Know...........31

Websites to Visit 31

About the Author 32

Atlanta Facts

Founded: 1837
Land area: 133.15 square miles (344.86 square kilometers)
Elevation: 1,050 feet (320 meters) above sea level
Previous names: Terminus, Marthasville
Population: 456,000
Average Daytime Temperatures:
winter: 54.3 degrees Fahrenheit (12.4 degrees Celsius)
spring: 72.7 degrees Fahrenheit (22.7 degrees Celsius)
summer: 87.7 degrees Fahrenheit (31 degrees Celsius)
fall: 73 degrees Fahrenheit (17.3 degrees Celsius)

Ethnic diversity:
African-American 54%
American Indian or Alaska Native 0.2%
Asian 3.1%
Native Hawaiian or Pacific Islander < .5%
Hispanic or Latino 5.2%
White 38.4%

City Nicknames:
The ATL
Hot'lanta
The Big Peach
Hollywood of the South

Number of Visitors Annually: 42 million

Where in the World?

Atlanta is located in the northwest part of the state of Georgia. Move your finger a little north on the map. You will touch the Blue Ridge Mountains. Curling around the northwest corner of the city is the Chattahoochee (Chat-uh-who-chee) River.

The Eastern Continental Divide runs through Atlanta. If precipitation falls on the west side of the line, the water drains into the Gulf of Mexico. If it falls on the east side of the line, the water drains into the Atlantic Ocean.

Atlanta has the highest elevation, or height above sea level, of any big city east of the Mississippi River. The highest part of the city, near Spelman College, is 1,073 feet (327.05 meters).

At 1,023 feet (311.8 meters), the Bank of America Plaza is the tenth tallest building in the United States.

Atlanta Notes

Dozens of streets in Atlanta are named Peachtree. Historians think it came from a Native American settlement named either Standing Peachtree or Standing Pitch Tree.

The End is the Beginning

Atlanta was created as the southern end of a railroad line that started in Chattanooga, Tennessee. In 1837, engineers from the railroad picked a spot. It was seven miles (11.3 kilometers) east of the Chattahoochee River. That's where Atlanta started. Being last in line is not always bad!

This railroad opened Atlanta to trade from the Tennessee and Ohio valleys.

Do you ever wonder how you got your name? Atlanta's first name was Terminus. This means end of the line. Then it was changed to Marthasville, the name of Governor Wilson Lumpkin's daughter. Finally, the name was changed to Atlanta in 1847. The name came from Atlantic, a nod to the Western and Atlantic railroad that started the town.

Wilson Lumpkin (1783–1870)

Atlanta Notes

Wilson Lumpkin was one of Georgia's most prominent political leaders during the antebellum period. After serving in local government and the state legislature, he was elected to Congress four times, serving 1815-17 and 1827-31. He resigned before serving his fourth term to run for the governorship of Georgia. Lumpkin was elected governor for two terms (1831-35).

Atlanta is the **capital** of Georgia. Forty-three ounces (1.22 kilograms) of gold cover the dome of the Georgia State Capitol building. Standing on top of the dome is a statue of Miss Freedom. She has a sword and a torch, so the gold is well protected!

Atlanta Notes
The Georgia State Capitol was named a National Historic Landmark and is listed on the National Register of Historic Places.

Miss Freedom is 22 feet (6.7 meters) tall from head to toe and weighs about 1,600 pounds (725.75 kilograms).

The Civil War

When the Civil War began in 1861, Atlanta became an important producer of munitions, or weapons. This made it a leading city for the Confederate forces. The Confederacy was a group of 11 southern states that wanted to secede, or leave, the United States in 1861. The remaining states were called the Union states.

Atlanta's **population** more than doubled during the war. The downside? It made Atlanta a target for Union forces.

Union states without slavery
Union States with slavery
Confederate States
Territories

The Civil War started because of disagreements between free and slave states over the rights of the government to prohibit slavery.

Do you want to win a war? Stop your opponent from getting supplies. This is exactly what General William Sherman of the Union Army had in mind in 1864. Sherman ordered the destruction of Atlanta. This would leave the Confederate Army without needed supplies. Buildings were burned. All of the railroads and depots were destroyed. Only $1.64 was left in the city treasury. Atlanta was left in ruins.

Atlanta Union Station was destroyed by General William Sherman and the Union Army in 1864.

On the Move

How do you make a comeback? If you are a city, it starts with transportation. Atlanta's strength was its railroads. All five were operating a year after their destruction in the war. By 1900, 15 railroad lines were coming through the city. The population grew from 20,000 people in 1865 to 90,000 people in 1900. Atlanta was building a reputation as the transportation **hub** of the Southeast.

The rebuilding of Atlanta's railway systems had a major impact on its population and economy.

On a Monday morning in 1917, four small fires started in Atlanta that quickly engulfed the city. Now known as The Great Atlanta Fire of 1917, the tragedy destroyed 1,938 buildings and left more than 10,000 people homeless.

Rising from the ashes, like the phoenix on the city seal, the city rebuilt again.

The official seal of Atlanta features a phoenix, a mythical bird that represents renewal and resurrection.

These days, Atlanta is a thriving, busy city. Hartfield-Jackson Atlanta International Airport served more than 96 million passengers in 2014. This topped all airports in the world. The terminal is as big as 45 football fields!

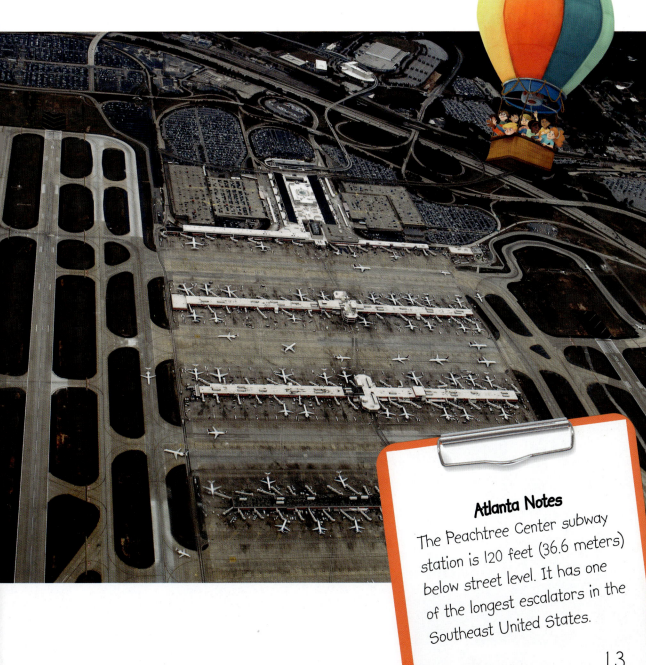

Atlanta Notes

The Peachtree Center subway station is 120 feet (36.6 meters) below street level. It has one of the longest escalators in the Southeast United States.

One of Atlanta's most unique buildings is the Fox Theater. Ballet Atlanta and Broadway shows **grace** the stage of this former movie palace built in 1929. The ceiling is a night sky with 96 embedded, or built in, crystal stars. One of the stars is a piece of a Coke bottle! Clouds are also projected across the ceiling. Ghosts are even believed to haunt the basement of the theater.

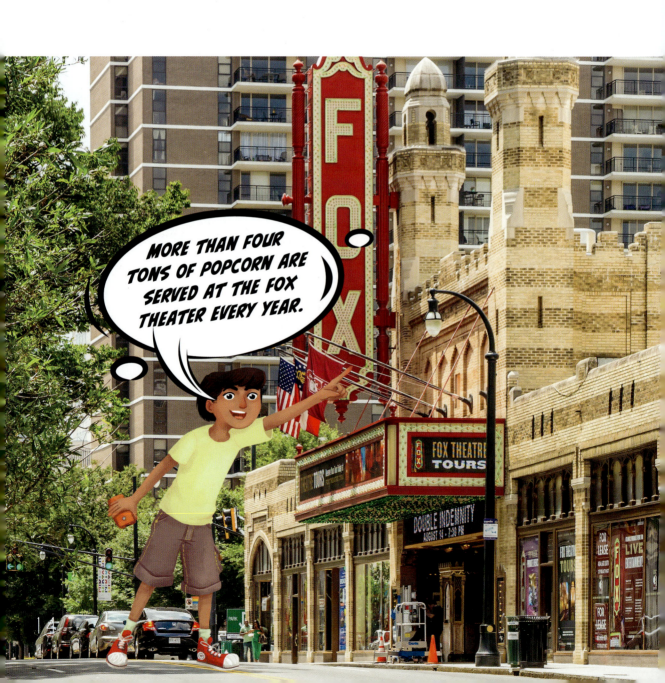

Famous Atlantans

In 1929, Martin Luther King Jr. was born in a two-story yellow brick house on Auburn Avenue. His father was the pastor of Ebenezer Baptist Church located on the same road. Auburn Avenue was a center of African-American culture during this time. In 1960, he became a co-pastor of Ebenezer with his father.

(1929–1968)

Martin Luther King Jr. was born and lived the first 12 years of his life in this home on Auburn Avenue. It is open for tours daily, except Thanksgiving, Christmas and New Year's Day.

Visitors can take a guided tour of King's childhood home. It is part of the Martin Luther King Jr. Historic Site. You can see **exhibits** illustrating King's life and legacy at the visitor's center. One of five designated

Peace Rose Gardens worldwide is located on the grounds. Visitors can view the tomb where Dr. King and his wife, Coretta Scott King, are buried.

Atlanta Notes

Atlanta's Fire Station No. 6, the oldest freestanding fire station in the city, is located at the MLK Historic Site. It was the first fire station in Atlanta to hire African-American firefighters.

The featured exhibit, "Courage To Lead," follows the parallel paths of Martin Luther King Jr. and the Civil Rights Movement.

Other historical figures also call Atlanta home. The Jimmy Carter Presidential Library and Museum is in Atlanta. Jimmy Carter was the 39th president of the United States. Maynard Jackson served as mayor of Atlanta for three terms. He was the first African-American to be elected mayor of a large southern city. Another Atlanta mayor, Andrew Young, also served as the first African-American United States ambassador to the United Nations.

Maynard Jackson (1938–2003) served two terms as mayor from 1974 to 1982 and another term from 1990 to 1994.

Andrew Young worked with Dr. Martin Luther King Jr. during the Civil Rights Movement.

Before becoming Governor of Georgia and U.S. President, Jimmy Carter was a peanut farmer in his hometown of Plains, Georgia.

Many celebrities are connected to Atlanta. Hall of Fame baseball player Henry "Hank" Aaron, played for the Atlanta Braves. He has been an **executive** with the team since retiring. Hank broke Babe Ruth's longstanding homerun record in 1974.

Margaret Mitchell, author of *Gone with the Wind*, was born in Atlanta. More than 30 million copies of this Civil War-era novel have been printed. You can visit her home in Atlanta.

Hank Aaron

In 1999, to celebrate the 25th anniversary of breaking Ruth's record, Major League Baseball announced the Hank Aaron Award, given annually to the best overall hitter in each league. Hank Aaron was honored with the Presidential Medal of Freedom in 2002.

City of Learning

Atlanta is home to many famous colleges and universities. Emory University has one of the best medical schools in the country. If you want to be an engineer, Georgia Tech could be the place for you. Or perhaps you're interested in a leadership role? The Atlanta University Center is the largest group of African-American private **institutions** of higher education.

The Tech Tower at Georgia Tech was built in 1888.

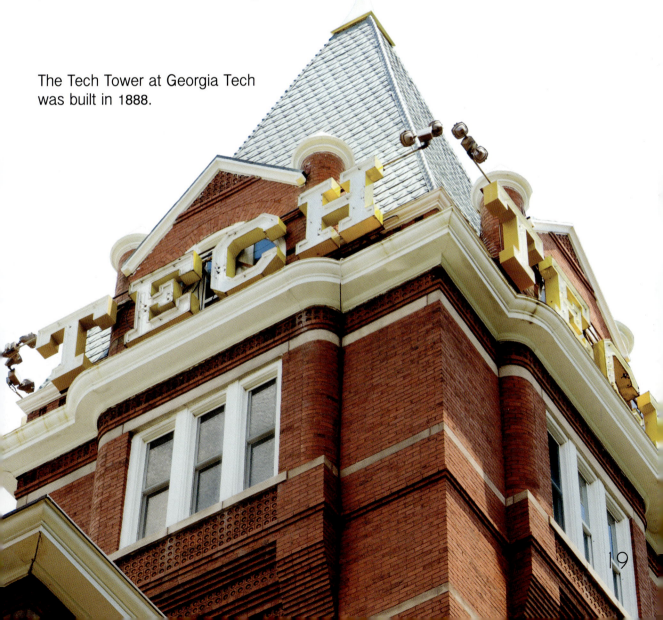

Games People Play

Atlanta is a sports town. Professional baseball's Atlanta Braves swat homeruns at Turner Field. They won the World Series in 1995. The National Football League's Atlanta Falcons play in front of more than 70,000 fans at the Georgia Dome.

The 27-story Georgia Dome is the second-largest domed structure in the world. It is a little over 292 feet (89 meters) tall.

The NBA's Hawks and WNBA's Dream also play in Atlanta. Atlanta Motor Speedway hosts more than 100,000 NASCAR fans to watch a 500-mile (804.7 kilometer) race. Soccer's Atlanta United football club will start in 2017.

Sixty thousand runners compete in the annual Peachtree 10K race. It's the largest 10K in the world.

Team	League	First year in Atlanta
Atlanta Braves	MLB	1966
Atlanta Falcons	NFL	1966
Atlanta Hawks	NBA	1968
Atlanta Dream	WNBA	2008
Atlanta United FC	MLS	2017
Atlanta Motor Speedway	NASCAR	1960

All eyes were on Atlanta when the city hosted the 1996 Summer Olympic Games. It lasted 17 days. More than 2 million people visited. Another 3 billion watched on television. It was the largest event in the history of the city.

Muhammad Ali lights the torch to open the 1996 Summer Olympic Games in Atlanta.

Hosting the games produced long-lasting **effects**. Centennial Park, built as part of the games, is a 21-acre (8.5 hectare) park that features an interactive fountain. The Fountain of Rings has jets of water and lights that operate in sync with the music that is played.

Grant Park started in 1882 with a gift of 100 acres (40.47 hectares). It was Atlanta's first modern public park. Now there are 248 parks and more than 3,000 acres (1,214 hectares) of park space. North of Atlanta, Lake Lanier supplies much of the city's water. It also provides many opportunities for **recreation**.

LAKE LANIER HOLDS ABOUT 637 BILLION GALLONS OF WATER. THAT WOULD FILL 9.1 BILLION BATHTUBS!

Food, Fun, and Festivals

The Varsity is the world's largest drive-in restaurant. It started in 1928 as a place for Georgia Tech students to eat. It is known for its hot dogs, car hops, and unique ordering language. Ask for a red dog and you will get a plain hot dog with ketchup. Shouts of "What'll Ya Have?" greet customers at the door or car window.

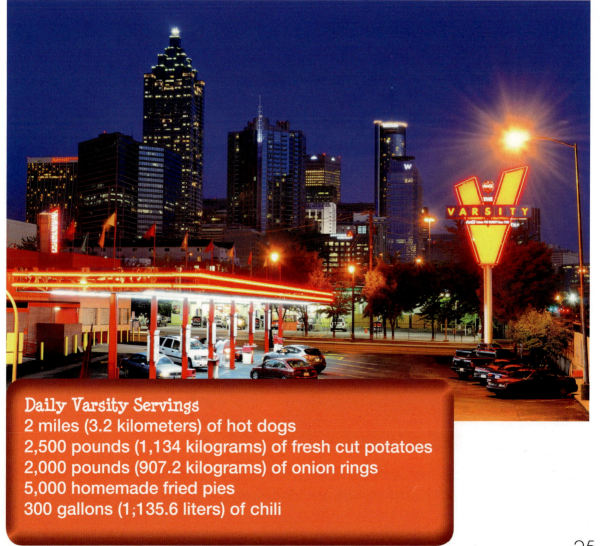

Daily Varsity Servings
2 miles (3.2 kilometers) of hot dogs
2,500 pounds (1,134 kilograms) of fresh cut potatoes
2,000 pounds (907.2 kilograms) of onion rings
5,000 homemade fried pies
300 gallons (1;135.6 liters) of chili

Atlanta's Tasty Invention

In 1886, John Pemberton, a pharmacist, concocted something new. He used parts of the coca leaf and the kola nut in a syrup. He mixed this with soda water. The first glass of Coca-Cola was sold at Jacobs Pharmacy in Atlanta. About 3,200 servings of Coca-Cola were sold that year. Almost two billion Coke products are now sold every day.

John Pemberton
(1819—1899)

At the World of Coca-Cola, exhibits display the history of the popular soft drink, and visitors are treated to unlimited samples.

Attendees of the famous Dragon Con gaming convention often dress up in their favorite character costumes.

Science fiction fans love Atlanta. More than 50,000 participants attend Dragon Con, the largest fantasy/science fiction convention in the United States.

Another festive occasion is Festival Peachtree Latino. It is the largest **multicultural** event in the Southeast. A live music stage features international performers.

Atlanta has been a little fishy since the Georgia Aquarium opened in 2005. It is the largest aquarium in the Western Hemisphere. Beluga whales swim overhead as you walk through a tunnel.

Atlanta Notes
The only place in North America to see a whale shark in captivity is at Atlanta's Georgia Aquarium. Whale sharks are the largest fish in the world.

Timeline

1821
Creek Indians surrender land that is now Metro Atlanta.

1847
Town of Atlanta is incorporated.

1864
Atlanta is burned by Union forces.

1865
Georgia Institute of Technology is founded.

1886
First Coca-Cola drink is sold at Jacob's Pharmacy.

1892
Atlanta Zoo is established.

1917
The Great Atlanta fire starts.

1959
City's population reaches 1 million.

1960
Public schools in Atlanta begin desegregation.

1970
Peachtree Road Race begins.

1973
Maynard Jackson becomes the first African-American mayor of Atlanta.

1992
The Georgia Dome opens; SunTrust Plaza and Bank of America Plaza are built.

1995
The Atlanta Braves win the 1995 World Series.

1996
Summer Olympics are held in Atlanta.

2005
Atlanta's airport is named the world's busiest.

Glossary

capital (kap-UH-tuhl): the city in a country or state where the government is based

effects (uh-fekts): the result of something

executive (eg-zek-yuh-tiv): someone who has a senior job in a company

exhibits (eg-ZIB-its): public displays of works of art, historical objects, or other items

grace (grayss): an elegant way of moving

hub (huhb): the center of an organization or activity

institutions (in-stuh-TOO-shuhns): large organizations where people work or live together

multicultural (muhl-ti-KUHL-chuh-ruhl): involving or made up of people from different races or religions

population (pop-yuh-LAY-shuhn): the total number of people who live in a place

recreation (rek-ree-AY-shuhn): the games, sports, and hobbies that people enjoy in their spare time

Index

Ballet Atlanta 14

Carter, Jimmy 17

Centennial Park 23

colleges and universities 19

Dragon Con 27

fire 12

history 6, 7, 9, 10, 11, 12, 15

Jackson, Maynard 17

Jacobs Pharmacy 26

King Jr., Martin Luther 15, 16, 17

Peachtree 5, 13, 21, 27

recreation 24

Sherman, William 10

transportation 6, 11, 13

Young, Andrew 17

Show What You Know

1. On what road will you find Dr. Martin Luther King's childhood home?

2. The Varsity asks you to create a new hot dog for their menu. What would you suggest?

3. What type of transportation might you use to travel in Atlanta?

4. How many times has Atlanta been destroyed by fire?

5. Why do you think leaders chose the phoenix as the city's symbol?

Websites to Visit

http://childrensmuseumatlanta.org

www.georgiaaquarium.org

www.nps.gov/malu/index.htm

About the Author

Jeff Barger is a second grade teacher who lives in North Carolina with his wife and two daughters. He likes dropping in on lots of things including doughnuts, gardens, football games, and libraries.

Meet The Author!
www.meetREMauthors.com

PHOTO CREDITS: Cover (tp): ©Ekaterina Novikova; cover (bottom), page 25: ©Sepavo; cover (bottom): ©Forty3zero; page 1: ©John Bilous; page 3: ©gio_banfi; page 4: ©DavidLiu; page 5, 7, 8, 9, 11, 13, 16, 28: ©nipponsan; page 6, 7, 10, 11: ©loc; page 8, 14, 15, 28: ©f11photo; page 9: ©Rainer Lesniewski; page 12: ©gemena communication; page 12 (bottom): ©abadonian; page 13: ©Tammygaffney; page 15, 17, 26: ©wikipedia; page 16: Nage1; page 16 (bottom): ©US National Parks Service; page 18: ©wickedgood; page 18: ©Edstock; page 19, 27: ©Rob Hainer; page 20: ©Ross Ensley; page 21: ©Gregory Kendall; page 22: ©APimages; page 23: ©Marilyn Nieves; page 24: ©RodClementPhotography; page 26: ©Joe Carillet

Edited by: Keli Sipperley

Illustrations by: Caroline Romanet

Cover design by: Jen Thomas

Interior design by: Rhea Magaro

Library of Congress PCN Data

Dropping in on Atlanta / Jeff Barger
ISBN 978-1-68191-404-6 (hard cover)
ISBN 978-1-68191-446-6 (soft cover)
ISBN 978-1-68191-484-8 (e-Book)
Library of Congress Control Number: 2015951570

Also Available as:
ROURKE'S
e-Books

Printed in the United States of America, North Mankato, Minnesota